Panty Games

Confessions of a slut wife and more

By Rebecca Tyger

For all you wild kitties

Contents

I.   Panty Game leads to so much more

I can't really tell my story without telling the story of my marriage first. I'm a 45-year-old brunette, about 5-foot-10 with long tan legs, curly brown hair that I sometimes straighten with a curling iron (date nights) and large, perky tits that my husband adores.

My husband? He's 48, Puerto Rican, very athletic and a great dad. This is the second go-around for both of us as our first marriages ended in flames. I think what love most about my husband is his love of having fun and his ability to poke fun at himself. He never minds looking silly popping up and dancing goofily during end credit movie to a TV show we've been watching or contorting his face horrifically just to make us all laugh. He's also very tender with me and supports all of my dreams.

He's my soul mate and I love him with all my heart.

But, besides being loving and a great father, the most obvious trait my husband displays is that he is always in the mood. I mean always. Sometimes I think it's just his DNA though he insists it has everything to do with me. He's actually pulled me close in church to tell me that he can think of nothing but eating me!

Can you imagine?

We have a great sex life, have had threesomes with other women, and even went to Hedonism on our honeymoon. When we first met he was extremely jealous, almost to the point where it was obsessive. But over the years he's done a total and complete 180.

For the last few years his main overriding fantasy has actually been for me to have sex with another man. At first I didn't think he was serious about it, you know, just bedroom talk. Then, over time, he convinced me that it's not just sex talk, but something that he wants to actually happen.

I played along here and there during various parties and flirtations that never really went anywhere but probably could have if I pushed things. And I was fine with that. A night of watching me flirt at a party would usually lead to some of the greatest sex ever. And I certainly never thought there was really any possibility if it coming true until the day he told me he had hired a surfing coach to give my son private lessons.

When Bradley walked through the door to meet us, I nearly lost it right there. He had short-cropped dark hair, dark skin like he was Italian or French, deep-set searing blue eyes and a body that came out of a bathing suit catalogue.

We live a literal stone's throw from the beach and the surfers in the area, well, the surfers just rock these incredible bodies all the time. Bradley was no different. Lean, muscular, abs and did I already mention gorgeous?

Was it my imagination or was he totally staring at me? I could feel myself blushing under the heat of his gaze and was wishing that he would look away.

I have never been attracted to younger guys, preferring the experience and expert touch of a more mature man, but this guy made my insides tingle almost instantly. I didn't care that he was 26 years old. I forced myself to look away and to remember that he was here to teach surfing, not to service me.

Or so I thought.

We sent Bradley to my son's room so they could meet and set up a schedule. I went to the bathroom to splash some cold water on my face when I instantly noticed that the red thong panties I had worn to the gym that morning were missing from atop the laundry basket. I had just placed my dirty workout clothes on the pile seconds before hearing the doorbell ring. I bent down to look for my panties but they were nowhere to be found. I moved the laundry basket to see if they had fallen behind it but there was nothing there.

Could Bradley have….no, of course not silly, I chastised myself for even thinking that way. I was old enough to be his mother.

But when he came out to say goodbye to us – and collect my husband's check – he had a devilish grin on his face and his eyes were once again burning through me. It was at that moment that I was dead-sure he had snatched my sweaty panties from the pile.

And I have to admit, the thought made me a little weak in the knees and instantly damp.

That night I shared my suspicions with my husband, who was more turned on than anything by my story. He held my arms down over my head and fucked me slow and hard, his hard throbbing cock pulsating in and out of my wet pussy as he made me recount meeting Bradley and discovering the missing panties over and over. He pulled my hair slightly, the way I like and sucked on my neck and fucked me harder and harder, increasing speed and ferocity with each thrust.

"Close your eyes," he whispered in my ear. "Pretend he's fucking you right now, the way you know he's rubbing his big hard cock on your panties and enjoying your scent."

Those words sent me over the edge. I dug my nails into my husband's back and thrust my hips straight up in the air to take him all in as I came. It was one of the most powerful orgasms I had ever had and from that moment on I could not stop thinking of Bradley and his six-pack abs and his hard cock and how brazen he had been in stealing my panties. I loved the thought that he was sniffing my panties to get himself off. I imagined his cum gushing out from the head of his cock and spilling out over the outside of his hands. I fantasized about cleaning every last drop off with my tongue.

Needless to say, I could barely wait for tomorrow when he would return to the house to take my son out surfing.

"You know what you should do," my husband suggested after shooting his hot, sticky cum all over my tummy. "You should make sure you leave another pair of panties on top of the laundry when he comes over tomorrow. If that pair vanishes then you'll know for sure and also know how much he enjoyed the first pair."

I thought it was a great idea. The following morning I attended a boot camp workout at the gym. I made sure to wear the sluttiest pair of panties I owned, straight from the Frederick's of Hollywood catalog. They were black, faux leather and tiny. I worked out especially hard, making sure I worked up a good sweat in them.

But I wanted him to have more. After I got him from the gym and sent the kids off to school, I climbed into my bed to make sure they would be perfect. I rubbed my tight, shaven pussy through my panties, only moving them to the side once to stick two fingers deep inside as I climaxed. I usually need some sort of penetration to get off but the thought of him wanting my panties sent me over the edge much quicker than normal. When I was done, I rubbed the panties more, nearly pushing them deep inside myself. If he wanted to enjoy my scent, then this was definitely his chance.

I showered and dressed, wearing a low-cut top that showed off my cleavage and placed the panties right atop the laundry pile once I heard the doorbell ring.

I let Bradley in and his eyes went right from mine to my tits and then my crotch before he even said hello. Normally I would have found this a bit unsettling but I knew he was young and still had a lot to learn. Plus, he really turned me on. It was is if he could make my pussy wet just by looking at it. I wanted him. I wanted him to take me, to control me, to eat me and to fuck me.

I fumbled over a few words before telling him to go back and get my son for their lesson and sure enough, moments later my panties were gone.

My heart started beating wildly. I felt nervous and excited all at the same time. I instantly imagined him smelling them, rubbing them on his face and chest, down to his tight abs and then down further to his cock. Oh, how badly I wanted to see his cock at that moment, to touch it and stroke it and taste it.

They left to go surf and I immediately called my husband to tell him.

"I'm not surprised," he said.

"You're not?"

"No, you're a sexy, fucking bitch."

"I love you."

"I love you too," he answered. "And, you know, as long as you tell me everything, every little detail, it would be OK with me if you wanted to, you know."

I did know, but I needed him to say it.

"Are you telling me what I think you are?"

"Yes, absolutely. You've let me fuck so many women over the years. It's time you enjoyed some new cock. Just don't do it behind my back."

"I don't know if I can," I lied.

"Oh please. I know you've already fucked him with your eyes."

"Ha, ha, you know me too well," I said. "I'll think about it."

As those words left my lips and I hung up the phone, Bradley had scampered back into the house to get a package of wax for the board.

"Should I come by tomorrow at the same time?" he asked.

"Yes, definitely," I answered nervously, knowing full well that my son worked at his part-time job directly after the school that day and my daughter had chorus. I would be home alone.

It was happening and I was excited and nervous all at the same time. My heart was racing. What on earth was I thinking?

I planned on calling him to cancel the appointment but my husband convinced me to go forward. How? During another great night of sex of course. This time my husband started by kissing my tummy and then spreading my legs lightly to taste my moist clit and slowly stick his index and middle fingers up into my cunt.

He lapped my pussy furiously, all the while thrusting his two fingers way up into me. All I could think about was Bradley doing that to me. As my husband could sense me tense my body to release everything I had, he pushed my bent knees back as far as they would go and stuck his tongue into my asshole.

I grabbed his hand squeezed so tight as I came that he had to ice his thumb later that night.

It felt so good that I kept his face and tongue there as I came for what seemed like an eternity.

"That's it," I commanded. "Eat my ass, eat me all up."

When I had finally had enough, I flipped him over and sucked his cock like it was the last night on earth. To repay the favor, I stuck my middle finger deep up into his cute ass as he was about to cum and he moaned like I had never heard before. He shuddered as he shot his load into my mouth and then pulled me up close to him immediately to kiss me, sucking back some of his lovely jism that he had just given me.

"Indian giver," I smiled.

"Mmm, yummy," he laughed.

Then he told me to keep the appointment with Bradley and to see where it went.

"What if it went as far as his cock in my pussy? You would be alright with that?"

"I would be more than alright."

"You swear?"

"Yes, I swear."

I started the following day like any other – at the gym. I needed to keep busy. Every idle moment found me fantasizing about riding Bradley's cock and scratching his gorgeous taut chest. The day dragged on and I was feeling desperate. Finally, 3 p.m. rolled around and I put on a little bit of eye liner and lipstick and timed his pressing of the doorbell perfectly with my emergence from the swimming pool. I was wearing a red bikini I had purchased for my honeymoon years before and was thrilled that the boot camp workouts and wheat-free diet had allowed me to wear it still.

Who am I kidding? I looked better now than I ever had. I was still dripping wet with pool water when I hurried in to answer the door.

"Oh Bradley," I acted surprised. "My son is not home yet. You're welcome to wait here in the living room of course."

His jaw had fallen open and he openly gawked at my body. I could feel every one of my muscles tighten and tingle with excitement. The only question now was whether I had the guts to go through with it.

He sat down and had to cross his legs to hide the growing prize waiting for me in his longboard shorts.

"Actually I'm glad you're here a little early," I found myself talking though I had no idea what was giving me the strength. It was now or never. Would I be able to cross a line that I would never be able to uncross? "I need to talk to you about something."

I walked over and sat on the arm of the love chair directly opposite him, knowing that at the right angle he might be able to get a peek at my pussy.

"I know what you've done," I said a bit sternly but not angrily.

He sat stunned and his eyes widened.

"What?"

"Don't play stupid. I know what private, personal items of mine you've taken."

"I…I…I didn't…"

I took a deep breath in. This was it. Moment of truth.

"And my only question to you is, if you wanted to smell and taste my pussy, why didn't you just ask?"

Not believing those words actually came out of my mouth, I realized. Had become increasingly wet and was worried about dripping down my leg. I could barely breathe or hear anything that was going on around me. I could feel my pulse way up in my ears which grew warmer by the second and I wondered if I had just made a total fool of myself.

I closed my eyes, dropped my head back and moved my bathing suit bottom off to the side, exposing my freshly shaven, glistening pussy.

I held my breath and waited. *Please, come fuck me, I pleaded in my mind.*

There was silence and my heart began to drop. How was I ever going to explain this to Bradley if I was mistaken. I would never be able to look him in the eye again. I would need to find a new coach for my son. What had I done?

But, just as I was about to drop my head in shame, I felt it. His breathing, heavy and louder coming closer. I could feel his breath on my thighs. Then it happened. His hands gently on my ass followed by his tongue devouring my eager, greedy cunt.

With my free hand I grabbed the back of his head and shoved his face deeper into me. With every flick of his tongue, every long lick, I fell deeper and deeper into ecstasy.

It was as if he knew me already, intimately and knew just what I wanted.

As he continued licking, he shoved his thumb into my pussy while carefully placing his middle finger on the entrance to my asshole. He circled it slowly, increasing the pressure until just the tip of his finger penetrated my asshole. I placed my hand over his and guided his finger deeper into my backside.

That caused him to push his face deeper into my cunt. The pressure from both sides, his tongue, his fingers, his lust for me caused me to come as hard as I ever had. I'm not a squirter but there was definitely some extra juices flowing down over his face.

I can't even remember how or when but we were soon out of the living room and into my bedroom with his deliciously hard cock fucking my mouth. When I could feel him getting too close, I backed off and just ran the tip of my index finger around the rim of his head and then over his slit, oozing with pre-cum. A few times I had to stop touching him all together. The last thing I wanted was for him to shoot his load before I could feel that beautiful cock deep inside me.

Although I have to admit that the thought of him filling my mouth with his hot, creamy, sticky drove me crazy. But I wanted more. I stopped as he was about to explode.

I backed off to let him recover and stroked his sweaty hair back on his head and kissed his beautiful face. His lips were full and soft and I could taste myself all over him.

Then I laid him down gently on the bed and very slowly started to squat over him. With my hands planted firmly on his chest, I lowered myself down as slowly as I could onto his throbbing dick. He moaned when the tip of his cock penetrated me and then I tantalizingly lowered my body all the way down and then right back up as slow as I could stand it. I rose up high enough for his cock to fall out of me. It glistened with my juices and I couldn't help but to lean over and lick it clean. Then I squatted a dozen more times slowly until he couldn't stand it.

He threw me off of him onto my back and lifted my ankles high into the air. Then he pounded me, showing no mercy until my entire body tightened and I let out a stifled cry as I came for a second time, this time all over his cock.

He took his hard dick out of me and buried his face in my cunt. He licked and lapped up all of my cum. He paused for a moment and kissed me tenderly before getting back to business.

Somehow his cock felt even harder than before. He didn't miss a beat. He continued thrusting and thrusting until it was time.

"Come inside of me," I whispered in his ear.

No sooner had I said that when his body shuddered and his hands dropped my ankles as he came violently deep inside me. I grabbed his ass and kept him in me until every drop was in my pussy.

He fell over on his back and saw a photograph of my husband on the nightstand.

"Oh gosh, I need to get the fuck out of here," he stammered. "That was incredible but I have to go."

"I understand," I relied with a smile.

Then I lay back on my bed and counted the minutes until my husband could come home and eat Bradley's cum out of my cunt. I could only dream of the punishments he would have in store for me for being such a naughty wife.

II.　　Cuckold Fantasy opens new door

When I first met my gorgeous and extremely sexy wife, she was coming off of a very bad breakup with the man who ultimately helped end her own first marriage. Turns out it was her husband's best man that she had fallen for and while she was drawn to his dark and wild sexual fantasies, he was never able to fulfill the tender, loving part that would have made it a lasting relationship.

His deficit was my gain as I came along just at the right time.

And while my wife has been nothing but giving to me sexually over the years with threesomes and fantasies and even flirtations and close calls with other couples, a part of me was always a bit insecure about her relationship with him. She often described it as physical and would say that he tried turning her into something that she wasn't.

Anyway, she remained very bitter about the breakup until he popped up one day on Facebook and started messaging her. I hid my jealousy as best as I could and then found something remarkable. Their expanding daily conversations – innocent mostly but bordering on the fringes of flirtation at times – were turning me on.

I found myself fantasizing to the thought of her fucking him, Steve. I would lie in bed, as she was getting ready for work, sometimes right after we had just fucked and I would picture her riding his hard cock. I would stroke myself hard again and slip a finger in and out of my asshole while I pictured my wife digging her nails into his chest and licking the sweat from his neck as she rode his shaft wildly. I pictured him exploding deep inside of her and for the first time in my life I pictured myself there to lick it all out of her.

Now, I had never until this moment in my life, ever thought of eating cum, not mine nor anyone else's. I knew I wasn't gay and never considered the possibility that I could be bisexual. So, just what was this new fascination I had with eating the cum from one of my wife's ex-lovers? In fact, before this, the thought of my own cum kind of grossed me out the second after shooting my load.

But now here I was , shooting my load thinking about his hot cum oozing back out of my wife's beautiful cunt and into my mouth. Sometimes I even pictured myself licking the tip of his cum-drenched cock. The fantasy was so good that, despite being slightly embarrassed, I could not keep it to myself.

Much to my wife's initial shock and her pleasure, soon the fantasy became a dual one.

I had just come out of the shower and was feeling pretty nice from the vodka tonics we had been drinking all night. I wasn't sure how she would take it if I brought it up but I was dying to try. She immediately took my cock in her mouth and started sucking me hard. She swirled her tongue around the tip of my cock and could tell it was driving me crazy. Then she very lightly started flicking the slit in my cock with the faintest touch from her tongue and I thought I was going to lose it. I thought that was my opportunity.

"Was that how Steve used to like it?" I asked.

She looked surprised and unsure how to take the question.

"I want you to show me how you used to suck his cock," I paused. "Pretend I'm him."

Those words seemed to set her off as she went down on me like I've never felt before. She lost all abandon and aggressively slurped, licked and sucked my cock to the point where I thought I was going to lose my load a lot sooner than I wanted to. I grabbed her shoulders and moved her away, needing her to stop.

Then I buried my face between her legs and was astonished at how wet her pussy was without me even touching her yet. I thrust a finger deep inside as I licker her then added a second finger and a third.

"Do you miss fucking him? It's ok if you do. It's more than OK if you do."

"Yes," she gasped as she grabbed my shoulders and started to climax. "I miss fucking him. I think about it a lot."

I stuck my tongue as far up into her snatch as I could and with that she shuddered and whimpered in a powerful climax. I let her catch her breath for a moment before I spoke up.

"Now, I want you to fuck me the way he loved you to."

She climbed on top of me and straddled my pulsing cock, moving her juicy pussy up and down. She looked away the entire time and I could tell she was thinking of him. She kept one hand on my my chest and with the other hand she rubbed her enormous tits.

Then, while still atop my throbbing member, she turned and faced the other way. She rode my cock reverse cowgirl and I could see her thick and creamy juices covering my cock. I loved seeing her asshole open and close with every thrust.

Finally, when my cock was covered in her milky, delicious juices, I couldn't stand it any longer. I exploded inside of her.

That was the start of it. Steve became a regular in our nighttime and sometimes morning fantasies. After a while I was comfortable telling her that I had been touching myself to the thought of eating his cum out of her.

"Why stop there?" She asked with a devilish grin.

"What do you mean?" I could feel my cock begin to ache.

"Wouldn't you like to see what his cock tasted like?"

My heart raced at the thought and my cock sprung to attention. I didn't know what to say. The answer was of course yes, a resounding yes, but I wasn't sure how Jen would take it. I started to kiss her instead of answering and then she allayed my fears.

"I would love to see you suck his big hard cock while I fucked you," she said, slipping her tongue in and out of my mouth gently. "I want to see your tongue lick it up and down and suck his head. Then I want to see him cum in your mouth. And trust me, Steve cums a lot."

By this time her hand was rubbing my cock through my pants.

"I would love to suck his cock," I confided. "And I would love to share that cum with you in a deep kiss."

Where was this coming from? Who was I becoming? I was terrified but exhilarated all at the same time. I wanted it. I wanted a man's cock in my mouth.

With that she got on her knees, unzipped my pants and took my throbbing member out of its confinement into the wonder of her mouth. She slurped and sucked, taking it out of her mouth only long enough to tell me how much she wanted to share Steve's cum with me. I let go and shot onto her face and mouth.

She immediately stood up and started kissing me, urging me to lick my own cum off her face and out of her mouth. I had no idea how deliciously exciting that would all be. I didn't hesitate in the least. I kissed her and licked her lips and chin. It was warm and thick and I knew I was already hooked.

It wasn't soon after that I encouraged her to get a little flirtatious on her Facebook messaging with Steve. He told her that he missed seeing her and the times they enjoyed together. Before long he had invited the both of us on his boat.

That was when Jen decided to let me in on a little secret that blew my mind: she used wear a strap-on dildo and fuck Steve in the ass.

"I wasn't really into it but I knew it brought him pleasure so I did it," she said.

"You used to peg Steve? Holy fuck. How did I not know this until now?"

I told her to ask him on Facebook if he had one on the boat. After much reluctance on her part and begging on mine, she agreed. That opened the door to all types of conversation and anticipation. Finally, the day of the arranged boating trip arrived.

We met Steve at the docks in Sebastian and he immediately shook my hand and seemed very friendly. He hugged and kissed Jen and I could feel a sexual spark ignite between the two right away. We went out onto the river and into the inlet to a private spot he knew about where we could anchor up, drink some wine and watch the sunset. It sounded perfect and it was.

The sun was high in the cloudless sky and the breeze coming up the Intracoastal waterway kept it comfortable.

The conversation was fun and intelligent and we all got along famously. After a few glasses of wine, Jen tends to get touchy-feely and soon she was caressing Steve's arms whenever he spoke. After an initial and unexpected pang of jealousy that I feared might derail the entire fantasy from ever becoming reality, I found that I was massively turned on.

Soon, she was holding his hand. He glanced over at me and I must have given him the signal that all was well because pretty soon he was caressing her arms and thighs as well. I scooched a little closer to them and started stroking Jen's hair when she spoke.

She turned to me and smiled and I gave her a deep tongue kiss.

"Wo, you two should get a room," Steve joked.

That was my opportunity to make the fantasy real.

"Oh, that's too bad. I was just thinking it might be your turn for a kiss," before I could finish my sentence, he took Jen in his arms and kissed the lips he hadn't in more than 10 years. I could hear her moan lightly as they kissed, their tongues darting in and out of each other's mouths ever so gently.

She looked at me with a devious grin and I undid the top of her bathing suit and deftly removed it, letting out her beautiful 38 D tits.

Steve reached up and pinched her nipple, causing her to moan louder. He rubbed it between his thumb and index finger making it harder than I had ever seen it get. She reached back and touched my erect cock through my bathing suit while she continued to kiss him. He slowly moved his hand from her nipple over her belly to the top of her bathing suit bottom where he lingered for a moment, caressing the area just below her belly button.

Then he slowly slipped his hand under the garment and onto her sopping wet completely shaven pussy.

He must have entered her with a finger because she let out a loud cry. I started kissing the back of her neck and she turned to kiss me on the mouth. I could taste Steve on her and I liked that. I moved to my knees and removed her bottoms, revealing Steve's greedy hand all over my wife's cunt. He fingered her tirelessly with his index and middle finger all the while his thumb was swirling around her clit.

Unable to stand it, she pushed his hands away and pulled down his bathing suit in one motion. He stood before her and his cock sprung up and slapped against her face. She opened her mouth and took it all. It was huge and beautiful.

I moved to my knees and started lapping up her gorgeous pussy lips and clit. When I could feel her getting close, I jammed two fingers in and she came in my face. She pulled me up closer to her and I knew what she wanted. It was what I wanted too. I just didn't know if it was what Steve wanted.

I had to trust her. She knew what he liked.

I inched closer and started kissing the side of her face as she continued sucking his cock. I could smell the excitement his cock was emitting. Her face was wet from his pre-cum and I licked it all as I kissed her, inching ever so close to her mouth and the prize that awaited me. Finally, when I could move no closer, she took his cock out and asked if I wanted to taste it.

I grabbed his cock and put it in my mouth without answering. What an odd sensation to have another man's cock in my mouth. Again, like before, I was terrific and exhilarated at the same time. When there was no objection from Steve, I really started to suck him off. His hot, throbbing dick felt awesome in my mouth. I took it out and licked the head all around and under his shaft from his balls to the head.

I put it back in my mouth and I stroked it with one hand while moving my other hand to his ass.

If he liked Jen fucking him with a dildo, then he would love what I had in store for him. I placed my middle finger right on his asshole and his knees buckled as I continued to suck. Ever so slowly I inserted my finger, deeper and deeper into his ass as he thrust his hips harder and harder into my mouth. His asshole was hot like fire and moist.

By this time Jen was lying down next to me sucking my cock. I was having so much fun that I barely noticed I was close to coming. I urged her to stop as I didn't want the fun to end yet. That was when Steve pulled his cock from my mouth and echoed my sentiments.

"But," I protested, "I really want you to cum in my mouth."

"Oh, I will," he said. "But I was hoping someone would fuck me in the ass first. I have a strap on for Jen to wear but now I have another idea."

Jennifer smiled at me and said "go for it."

I leaned Steve over and kissed his back, moving down to his ass. I spread his cheeks apart and started darting my tongue in and out of his asshole. It tasted better than it had felt.

"If you promise not to cum, I'll suck your cock until John is finished."

I ate his asshole like there was no tomorrow. Then, when it was good and wet, I carefully placed my cock near his hole and sent it in. His asshole was so tight and gorgeous, I nearly exploded the second I stuck it in. Steve moaned as I increased my thrusting.

"Fuck me," he yelled. "Fuck me with that cock."

I felt weak in the knees. It was like a dream. I followed his instructions while Jen continued sucking him off. Finally, unable to stand anymore, I exploded deep into his ass with a shudder.

As soon as I did, he turned around and his cock was in my face. I sucked for a moment and then could feel the hot sticky jism fill my mouth. I swallowed some down so I would not gag and then kissed Jen. We shared the cum back and forth between the three of us.

The fucking and sucking continued throughout the night. Jen got to wear her strap-on after all and fucked the both of us. We took turns fucking her and filling her with cum. Steve gladly licked my load out of her and I returned the favor later on.

The highlight of the night was when Jen laid us down with our heads on opposite ends of the bed and was able to sit on both of our cocks at the same time. She rode us until we both creamed inside of her.

But that experience is worth a story unto its own.

Needless to say boating has become our new favorite hobby.

III. Let me sniff those festive panties

It was a Christmas party I will not soon forget. My husband's band was playing and raising money for a local homeless shelter and all of our friends were there getting nice and tipsy on beer and wine. I was dressed in a seductive black mini dress that accentuated my curves and heels. I dressed sexy that night because I was feeling sexy.

With the holiday craziness and our children coming back from college, it had been a few weeks since my husband and I were able to enjoy a little one-on-one time. But now I wanted some. I needed it. I told my husband not to make the Christmas party an all-night affair because my desired needed tending to.

By my third glass of wine I was feeling really good and by my fourth all I could think about was getting my husband home and inside of me. My panties, black thongs from Frederick's of Hollywood, were already feeling moist. I decided that it was time for them to come off. I went to the bathroom and removed them. They were wetter than I had anticipated and they smelled strongly of my desires.

During one of the band's breaks. I dragged my husband over to a dark corner and gave him a deep kiss.

As he was kissing me back, forced something into my hand. He knew right away what it was: my tiny, yet sopping wet panties. He's told me all about his panty fetish and how sometimes he'll fetch my dirty panties from the hamper at home and inhale my musky aromas while he jerks off. He's even confessed to searching for panties at our friend's homes and sometimes being lucky enough to find a pair to smell.

Instead of feeling angry or betrayed, the idea of him sniffing another woman's dirty panties really got my juices flowing as well. I'd secretly hoped that he would share a pair he'd found with me. While I've never enjoyed the company of a woman in that way, the idea always turned me on. Threesomes with another woman were usually the topic of our sexual fantasies.

The fantasies always began with another woman's panties. He would find them and smell them and then then hold it to our faces while we fucked. It would give us the courage we'd need to seduce the other woman and we would enjoy every bit of her.

Of course, it was only a fantasy. But a damned good one.

So, here we are in a darkened corner of a Christmas Party and I'm kissing my husband like a teenager. Without care, he moved his hand, holding my balled-up panties to his face and started deeply breathing in my gorgeous pussy juices.

"Are you pleased with me?" I asked him seductively and leaned forward just enough t flash him my 38D breasts that were barely staying in this little black dress.

"Yes, very," he replied and went in to bite my lower lip.

"Good. Because I need you to take care of me tonight."

"That will not be a problem," he smiled and I could feel the erection in his pants swell. That was also the moment I noticed that a friend of ours – Tara -- a cute tattooed theater geek that we had been in a community theater production with once, had been sitting on the couch right next to us the entire time.

In our defense it was pretty dark.

"Don't let me stop you," she smiled and her tongue just faintly licked her bottom lip for a split second.

Now, I have to confess that I had fantasized about her a few times during our panty-sniffing threesome fantasies. Maybe it was because I wasn't sure she was straight or gay. She wasn't beautiful but there was something about her that made my pussy itch. Do you know what I mean? Maybe it was the tattoos or the piercings or maybe it was her perfectly round perky tits.

I always imagined that her nipples and clit were pierced and on more than one occasion I finished myself off in the shower picturing her. It was a good fantasy. And now here she was, licking her bottom lip and watching my husband smell my panties. I probably should have been mortified but thanks to the wine and my extremely horny state, I was excited.

When my husband and I fantasized about her while fucking, my husband would whisper to me how much he would love to lick Tara's pussy and wondered if there were any tattoos down near it. He would tell me how much he would want to kiss me after making her cum so I could taste it all.

He would describe in excruciating detail how she would then squeeze his cock tightly, flick her tongue on the tip and put it deep into her tight, wet pussy. I'd respond by telling to pretend he was fucking her and order him to cum deep inside of her so I could lick it all out. I'd tell him I would watch the cum drip down out of Tara's cunt into her ass and then dive in.

That usually got him to shoot his hot sticky load right then and there. I mean, he can only take so much, right?

You could only imagine my excitement and what my imagination was doing when I heard her voice only a few feet away from my exposed pussy and my hubby's raging hard-on. The things is, my imagination was nowhere even close to where things were going to go.

Tara's eyes did not move from my husband's pulsating cock and she only giggled when I slid my hand down to grip hs cock through my jeans in front of her. It definitely had to be the wine, right?

"I bet those panties smell yummy," Tara whispered to my husband. "Can you share?"

My heart started racing. My husband looked up at me with a mischievous grin but also to seek permissions. I lowered his hand to Tara's face, careful not to let everyone at the party see what was going on. She moved in and took a deep breath. Then without asking she took them from his hand and held them up to her face and inhaled deeply.

I gasped and clutched my husband's arm tightly. I could have cum right then and there.

Tara smiled and licked the gusset, the tiny patch of panty where my shaven pussy had been just moments before leaking sensuous juices. I'm sure it was still warm from my excitement.

"Hey, do you want to get out of here with us?" I stammered not sure how my husband was going to get out of playing a second set with his band.

Then as if reading my mind, Tara looked up at me and stared into my eyes, making me weak. She grinned devilishly.

"Yes. I think I've had way too much to drink and I need you to take me home. Is there any way that you can give me a ride?" She winked at both of us.

"Oh, we'll be giving you a ride alright," I don't know how the words came out of my mouth but they felt so right.

We said our goodbyes and hurried to the car. I pulled Tara into the back seat with me. She wore round little glasses and had several piercings up and down her ears and piercing in her nose and her tongue.

She wore an army camouflage mini-skirt with a man's white dress shirt on top. Her black nylons were stylishly ripped with large holes and she wore combat boots. Her hair was buzzed on one side and longer on the other. I Couldn't think of anything else but being with her.

The second my husband drove the car around the corner, we were kissing. I had never kissed another woman and it was everything I had hoped. It was soft but firm and purposeful. We stopped for a moment and smiled at each other. I moved the hair from the side of her face and kissed it gently. I was feeling especially emboldened.

"This isn't fair you know," I said.

"What's not fair?" she smiled and kissed me deeply.

"That you've gotten to smell my panties but I haven't smelled yours." Then I kissed her neck gently and moved my hand between her legs. She parted them for me and I reached up to stroke her pussy through her panties and pantyhose. She moaned gently and kissed me back. Her body seemed to go limp as I caressed her. She was mine.

"I'll give them to you the second we get to my place," she managed to whisper.

She lived only three miles from the party and we didn't even notice the car had stopped in Tara's driveway until my husband reached back around and put a finger deep inside of me. I nearly came right at that moment.

"Should we move this inside?" he eagerly asked.

We stumbled from the car, up her walkway and I kissed my husband deeply while she fumbled for her keys. It seemed to take forever for her to unlock the door and let us in. I had never wanted anything or anyone so badly in all my life. I felt so predatory and so vulnerable at the same time.

As soon as we were in her house, I pushed Tara up against the inside of her door and kissed her with my hand planted firmly between her legs. I could feel how hot and wet she was getting and I couldn't wait to hold those warm, moist panties to my face.

"Maybe we should get more comfortable," came the rare voice of reason from my husband as he undid the buckle of his belt. His cock must have been throbbing with anticipation knowing what was to come.

Tara giggled and grabbed my hand. She led us through her small, neat home to her bedroom. It was obvious she wasn't expecting company tonight and there were clothes strew about like a frat house.

My husband spotted them right away. Rolled up panties right beside a pair of running shorts and running shoes. He reached down and held them up to his face.

"Oh my God. These smell incredible," he said, holding his hand out to me.

I closed my eyes and inhaled them while my husband kissed Tara deeply on her lips. He moved slowly down her neck and then started unbuttoning her blouse. No one would ever believe that we had never had a threesome before. But it was playing out just as we had imagined in our fantasies.

He had no trouble removing her small light blue bra and her perfectly round tits stood firm before him. He reached his hand out and gently caressed her breast, slowing down to run the back of his hand over her engorged pink nipples. Was surprised at how much I was enjoying watching him in action. He kissed her face again and this time continued down her neck to her gorgeous tits. He sucked on her nipples and I could hear her gasp and try to catch her breath.

Clearly frustrated and in need of help, he pulled Tara's hand to the enormous bulge in his pants. She looked at me for approval before gripping his clothed cock in her hand.

Having enjoyed her used panties long enough, I was ready to taste the real thing. I glided behind her and kissed the back of her neck and ran my hands through her hair. Touching the buzzed crewcut section of her hair turned me on like crazy.

I could see her unzipping my husband's pants and pull his cock out. He clumsily pulled the pants completely off. It was surreal to see another woman's hand wrapped around my man's cock. I dropped slowly to my knees and kissed the small of Tara's back while unzipping her camouflage miniskirt.

I could already smell the sweaty, pungent prize waiting for me between her legs.

I pulled the skirt down and then started untying her black combat boots. Once relieved of those, I gently guided her to her bed where she lay on her back. My husband, not missing a beat, stood off to Tara's left and put his cock in her mouth. It was absolutely beautiful to see.

I kissed Tara's feet through her pantyhose and moved up her shins, to her thighs and then finally kissed her pussy through the hose and panty. The smell was strong and sweet and I immediately peeled her pantyhose off. She lifted her rear off the bed to help me.

Then I did the same with her drenched panty. I held it to my face and then gave to my husband who was in absolute heaven with Tara slurping and sucking his cock, like someone who knew exactly how he liked it.

I kissed Tara's pierced bellybutton and then slowly moved my face down over her stubbled mound.

"I'm sorry," she gasped, giving my husband's cock a break, "I would have shaved completely and made it all pretty if I knew something like this was going to happen."

"Sorry? This is absolutely perfect," I answered and then I lowered my head further and kissed a pussy for the first time in my life. It was soft and velvety and infinitely more delicious than I could ever have imagined. I kissed and sucked gently on her clit and then started instinctively running my tongue up and down her lips and slightly into her tight, little hole.

Before too long I felt her hand on the top of my head keeping me in a certain spot. Her body began to tense and I knew she was getting close. I slipped my middle finger up into her slippery cunt and her body became rigid as she moaned desperately. Her orgasm seemed to last forever and I continued licking, sucking and fingering the entire time.

She heaved and breathed loudly before giving me her signature devilish grin. I knew exactly what that smile mean. It was my turn. I stood quickly and turned my back so my husband could unzip my dress and undo my bra.

Tara looked genuinely astonished when she saw my tits. She grabbed me and pulled me onto her so she could suck them greedily. Seeing my husband's rigid cock covered in precum was nearly too much for me. I pulled him close and licked all of the juice from his cock then kissed Tara gently with it all.

We took turns kissing his cock and he pulled away after a short bit.

"Not yet," he seemed to hiss. "Not yet. I can't cum until I fuck that pussy."

Tara giggled.

"Is it OK for my husband to fuck you?" I teased.

"Hmm, I guess so, but only while I eat your pussy."

Her words made me wetter than before, which I would have thought impossible. I was almost embarrassed at how wet I was but all fears vanished when I felt her hot tongue devour me from the inside. Clearly this was not the first woman she'd been with.

She'd positioned herself on her hands and knees between my legs. My husband stood there jerking his cock while staring at her exposed ass and pussy. The room smelled of sex.

I cocked my head to the side so I could watch my husband in action. He pushed his face into Tara's ass and licked her asshole like there was no tomorrow. He alternated between licking her pussy and her asshole and I couldn't blame him one bit. Not only was she delicious but who knew if we would ever have this opportunity ever again.

I could hear her moaning as his magic tongue did its thing.

Then I heard her whisper a squeal as he slid his pulsing cock slowly into her. Knowing my husband, he only out the tip in for a moment, just pushing the head in and out slowly a dozen times before thrusting himself deep inside of her.

I watched him move his muscular body behind her and then I watched her face as she lifted her head from between my legs in just pure joy and ecstasy.

"I'm getting close," my husband said between breaths.

"Cum inside me," Tara answered. "Please cum inside me."

At that my husband let out a groan as he emptied his load deep inside of her. Once satisfied she returned to eat me and bring me to orgasm with her tongue and her fingers.

We collapsed in a sweaty, sultry heap of the bed, all three of us. My husband continued kissing her and I could tell they were both getting riled again. But there was something I wanted to try -- something that I'd always wanted to try in fact – before I could let him fuck ger again.

I moved my head down to the foot of the bed and moved one my legs under her body. Then I shimmied myself higher up on the bed until our pussies touched each other's. She pushed her pelvis down toward me and we started grinding our gaping, hungry, drenched pussies together all the while she kept kissing my husband.

The feeling was indescribable. We would stick together and become one and then keep mashing ourselves into each other. At one point, a thick glob of my husband's cum leaked out of her and served as a wonderful, hot sticky lubricant that our pussies shared with each other.

I wanted to cum again and closed my eyes as Tara and I moved in perfect unison creating this suction and a sound and smell that could only described as pure lust. It wasn't long before we both shuddered at the same time.

I though the night, as perfect as it had been, was over. Wrong. Watching us scissor each other had given my husband an enormous raging boner. He didn't wait, he didn't ask. He pulled Tara toward him, held her ankles in the air and entered her.

He slowly brought her feet to face and kissed and licked them the entire time his cock was thrusting its way in and out of her. My husband loves to slow-fuck and this was tantalizingly slow. The full length of his cock, covered in her creamy juices mixed with mine would slide all the way out and then he would re-insert it and send it all the way back in.

It wasn't long before I found my hand had made its way down between my legs. I had become insatiable.

Thankfully that first experience with Tara led to many more adventures with her and with others.

IV. The Start of it all

What's funny to me is that my introduction to the life of a hot wife might not have ever happened if my husband and I had bailed on a party neither of us wanted to attend.

It was during the holidays and there was still so much to do and we had already attended so many parties that we were looking forward to spending that December Saturday night at home, drinking egg nog, watching Christmas movies and fucking our brains out.

Up until that night we enjoyed a healthy and pretty spectacular sex life with each other. Our time together regularly included slutty lingerie, sex toys, oral and even anal on a few occasions. (Luckily, my husband prefers my pussy to my ass.) They also included a pretty healthy fantasy life. I fantasized about watching him fuck my friends and vice versa. If I wanted to get him off in a hurry I knew that I only had to mention how much I wanted to fuck one of his friends and he would explode.

I loved how much it turned both of us on but we never expected it would go further than extremely hot bedroom talk. Still, on more than one occasion my husband told me that he would absolutely love it if I actually fucked someone else and told him about it. Sometimes the fantasy went further. He would talk about wanting to lick another guy's load from my pussy and show me by cumming in=side me and then going down on me to gobble it all up.

We were also pretty adventurous, or so I thought. We'd often move our swimsuits to the side and fuck in the ocean. On more than one occasion I dragged him into the fitting room at a department store in order to service me and that fear of getting caught always caused me to climax quickly and violently.

Yep. We had a great sex life, or wo we thought, until that fateful night.

"Do we have to go to this Christmas party tonight?" I whined around four that afternoon with a tall glass of Chardonnay in my hands.

"Starting early?" he laughed, flashing that killer smile that always drove me nuts.

A little bit about us. We are both in our early 40s, both professionals and do our best to stay in decent shape. We each have two kids from previous relationships and so every other weekend we are kid-free.

My husband is tall with the physique of a soccer player. His dark hair matches his eyes, which, for as long as I've known him, have had a power over me. I am 5-10, have long dark hair, green eyes and long tan legs that my husband says he can stare at for eternity. My breasts are 36D with very little sag. My husband says that it's tough to pick out my best feature alternating on a regular basis between my eyes, ass, legs and boobs.

"Well, if you're already drinking then I'm gonna pour myself a bourbon," he said and walked over to the "holiday" bar we set up every year by the tree and collection of Nutcracker figures.

"You haven't answered my question. Do we really have to go tonight?"

"I think so...Dave already sent a text to my phone letting me know how excited he and Candice are to see us later on. Are you feeling party burnout?"

"Yeah, that and..."

"What?" he answered.

"Well, we're gonna have the kids and then company and you know what the holidays are around here. Tonight is our last night alone for the next few weeks and I thought we could, you know..."

That all-too-familiar glint came to his eyes and he started over to me.

"That sounds amazing....but....I already promised Dave," he said still smiling and looking sexy as ever. "However, I could be convinced to use the kids as an excuse why we needed to leave early, like super early."

With that I dropped to my knees in front of him and unbuckled the belt to his jeans. I slid them down slowly and pressed my face against the growing cock fighting to get out of his black boxer briefs. I could swell that musky sweet scent of excitement and t literally made my mouth water.

"Was this what you had in mind?" I asked as I gently pulled his cock to freedom and pursed my lips to kiss the precum forming at the tip. I looked up at him for an answer with a string of precum still connecting my lips to his bulging cock.

He nodded quietly and threw his head back as I didn't wait for his reply. I kissed the head of his wet cock over and over, incorporating my tongue only after my lips were covered in precum.

I edged and teased his cock, running a finger over the head and holding it up for him to see how wet he made my finger. I then ran that finger under his balls to his ass and inserted it slowly as I took more of his delicious cock into my mouth. He gasped as I fingered his ass faster and deeper while not missing a beat of his thrusting pelvis send his cock into and out of my mouth.

He lifted one leg up onto the couch allowing me to get deeper with my finger. I knew it wouldn't be long now. And like clockwork, there it was. His body tensed and he made guttural sounds just before sending his thick, creamy loud into my mouth. I looked up at him and made eye contact while I slurped down every last drop. Then, and only then did I slowly remove my finger from his asshole.

"OK, I finally managed to say. We go to the party, make an appearance, have a drink or two tops, then you take me home and have your way. Deal?"

"Oh my God," he was still recovering. "Anything. Anything at all...yes...yes of course."

"Good."

I took his flaccid cock in my hands and put it back into my mouth. Within seconds it started getting hard once more. I'm always amazed at the short amount of bounce back time my husband needs. It's like he's always ready for action.

I sucked on it gently and then put it back in its boxer briefs.

"That's just so you won't forget," I smiled and stood up before heading to the shower.

We'd been married for more than 10 years but showering that night, especially after sucking him off, made me so horny that I seriously considered making myself come in the shower. I actually started to but then took a deep breath and backed off knowing full well that he would take care of my needs later that night.

I was feeling sexy, wild, adventurous, horny and just a little frustrated while picking out my outfit for the party. I wanted something that would drive my husband wild all night.

I settled on my short black cocktail dress, a pair of black crotchless panties and a strappy pair of silver, glittery shoes. I guess I was going for classy stripper or call girl. Christmas in Florida means stockings are not necessary, which was perfect with me. I was already so wet, I wanted the freedom of having my long legs exposed to the fresh air.

My husband's jaw dropped when he saw me.

"Maybe we *should* skip that party after all. Jesus, look at you..." He walked over and out his strong hands on my waist and pulled me in for a kiss. As usual his hands began to wander and it wasn't long before his fingers discovered the slit in my panties. He sank his middle finger deep inside.

"What's this?" he asked devilishly.

"Mmm, just in case we don't want to wait until we get home from the party," I replied then slowly removed his hand from my shaven pussy before reaching the point of no return.

I knew that just knowing I was wearing crotchless panties would keep him from thinking about anything else all night. We got to the party around 7:30 and were already a bit buzzed from the drinks we had at home before going out. We sat in the driveway for a moment before going in and he leaned over and kissed me deeply. As he did, my husband slid his hand between my legs and eased his middle finger deep up inside me. I gasped and he smiled.

"Just wanted to give you a taste of what's to come. Let's go inside."

I was so worked up that by the time we entered the beautiful home on the intracoastal, I was already thinking about leaving.

My husband went off to see some of his buddies and I cozied up to some of the women in front of the tapas and near the wine. I poured myself a cold chardonnay and the heat from my husband's finger finally started to ease. I'm not a big drinker so the wine at home and now at the party started to affect me. Needless to say I was feeling pretty good.

After about an hour of listening to women complaining about their husbands or their kids or their exes, I glanced over to see if I could make eye contact with my husband. I was getting horny again and I wanted to give him the "hey, let's get out of here" look.

But he was in deep conversation and didn't notice. That's when I noticed another man staring at me. I didn't recognize him. He was a bit older, in great shape, with dark hair and black eyes. He raised his glass to me from across the room and I smiled awkwardly back.

I turned back toward the women but for reasons I still cannot explain, I could not stop thinking about him. He had that look. The look that says "I'm important. I'm wealthy. I get what I want and everyone knows it."

Plus, did I mention he was gorgeous?

I turned to look for my husband again but all I saw was this stranger's eyes staring right back at me. I looked away quickly. I felt guilty, nervous and excited all at once. His stare just unnerved me and made me weak in the knees. Or was it the wine?

Whatever it was I couldn't stop thinking of him. I could feel myself getting wet and with my crotchless panties I was literally afraid I would start dripping down my leg.

Another 20 minutes went by and every time I tried to get my husband's attention, I would inevitable lock eyes with the black-eyed stranger. And with every look I got wetter and wetter. I thought about what it would be like to have him inside me.

"OK, enough is enough," I told myself. "I'm going to use the restroom and then just tap my husband on the shoulder and tell him we needed to go."

I excused myself from the other ladies and when I noticed two people waiting for the downstairs restroom, I decided to use the upstairs bathroom. My friend wouldn't mind.

As I walked up the stairs I wondered if he was staring at my ass. I imagined him trying to sneak a peek up my short dress. I imagined his cock getting harder the second he glimpsed my wet pussy.

The was relieved to see the bathroom was empty. In fact, no one was upstairs. I entered and turned to close the door when the stranger's hand kept me from closing it.

He entered the bathroom without saying a word and closed the door behind him. I was paralyzed. I was wet. I tried to protest but instead allowed him to kiss my mouth deeply, his tongue darting in and out and around my bottom lip. He bit it gently and my legs turned to jelly. He turned me facing the sink and he kissed my neck from behind, staring at me in the mirror the entire time. He devoured me and I let him. His hands cupped my breasts and I lost my breath.

What was I doing? I knew it was wrong but I couldn't bring myself to stop it. He turned me back around and in one swift movement had two fingers deep up inside my wet pussy. He finger fucked me roughly, thrusting his fingers in and out of me furiously.

After only 20 seconds I started cumming all over his hand. I pulled him close as I climaxed and pulled his tongue into my mouth. Then he pulled his fingers out and held them up to my mouth. I eagerly licked my cum off of them, wanting to do anything to please him. I kissed him again and reached down to touch his cock. I rubbed and grasped at it through his pants.

It wasn't enough. I wanted to see it, to feel it, to taste it. I dropped my knees and pulled his pants down to the floor. His beautiful cock was enormous. It seemed to be bulging and throbbing. I gobbled it up immediately, alternating between sucking it and licking the shaft up and down.

He held it in his hands and smacked it against my face several times. My face was covered in precum. He pulled me up and licked my face. Then once again eh turned me around to face the mirror over the sink. He reached down and lifted my right leg up over the sink and he sank his enormous, rigid cock deep up inside me from behind.

I opened my eyes and found him staring at me in the mirror as he fucked me wildly. I kept my eyes open as best as I could and stared right back at him. They penetrated me just as his thick cock did. He fucked me with the perfect rhythm, slowly and deeply at first and then picking up in pace. I knew he was getting close to cumming when he stuck his fingers in my mouth.

He groaned slightly as he shot his hot, thick, sticky cum deep into me. I could feel wave after wave enter me as his cock pulsed and pulsed. He breathed heavily and kissed my neck over and over. I could feel his cock growing hard once again.

I pulled away.

"I'm...I'm sorry. I need to go," I whispered and exited the bathroom in one motion. I ran down the stairs and in a flustered state of shame and guilt told my husband that we needed to go.

He was in mid conversation about his fantasy football team and so he wasn't too pleased about leaving.

He started the car and started heading home when I told him to pull over. I confessed to him what had just happened, knowing full well I could never live with keeping that secret from him.

"Was it consensual."

"Yes, I'm afraid so," I answered.

"Did you enjoy yourself?"

I looked down and couldn't answer.

"It's OK," he continued. "Did you enjoy it?"

"Yes." I could feel my face getting hot.

"Did he cum inside you?"

"Yes."

"Is it still inside you?"

"Yes, I didn't have time to…"

I hadn't even finished the sentence by the time he was pushing me back and hiking up my dress. He buried his face between my legs and greedily lapped at my swollen, used pussy. I could feel the stranger's cum begin to ooze out and my husband ate me more ferociously.

He lifted his head and smiled at me. His mouth was covered in cum.

It was the sexiest thing I'd ever seen. I kissed him and reclaimed what was rightfully mine. And that, for us, was the start of everything.